Spider-Man Versus Doc Ock

Adaptation by Acton Figueroa
Illustrated by Jesus Redondo, Ivan Vasquez,
and the Thompson Bros.
Based on the Motion Picture
Screenplay by Alvin Sargent
Screen Story by David Koepp and Alfred Gough & Miles Millar
Based on the Marvel Comic Book by Stan Lee and Steve Ditko

🎬 HarperFestival®
A Division of HarperCollinsPublishers

Sometimes I do not know what is harder: being a hero or being a student.

When I am Spider-Man, I help others.

But sometimes I need help, too.

Like today—I am late for class again.

I do not want to be late for this class.

Dr. Connors is the professor.

I like him a lot.

I wish I could tell him why I am always late, but no one can know that I am Spider-Man.

After I run into him, Dr. Connors
reminds me that I have to write a
big paper for his class.

I am going to interview a scientist named Dr. Octavius.

He is performing a very dangerous experiment today.

I know all about danger.

Helping mankind is my

after-school job.

As my Uncle Ben said,

"With great power comes great

responsibility."

Helping people feels good.

I think that Uncle Ben
would be proud of me.

I do not get nervous when I am
saving people.

I do not have time.

I just go to work.

This is the fun part.

My job as a photographer is fun, too.

Working at the newspaper means
I always get the news before
anyone else.

Doc Ock?

That is a funny name.

It sounds a little like Dr. Octavius.

I hope that nothing went wrong with

his experiment.

I better take my paycheck to the bank now.

Yikes!

I am not the only one with
superpowers at the bank.

That is not the right way to make a withdrawal!

I think it is time for Spider-Man to help these people . . .

. . . before Doc Ock takes off

with all the cash!

He is ready for a fight and so am I.

Let's go!

You missed me, Doc Ock!

Ready or not, Doc Ock, here I come!

Fighting someone with four extra limbs is not easy.

My spider-strength comes in
handy at times like this.

Be careful on the way down!

Doc Ock is gone for now,

but he will be back.

And I will be waiting for him,

protecting the people of this city.

That is what a hero does.